CONTENTS

When the champions of Earth came together to battle a threat too big for a single hero, they realized the value of strength in numbers. Together they formed an unstoppable team, dedicated to defending the planet from the forces of evil. They are the . . .

{ ROLL CALL }

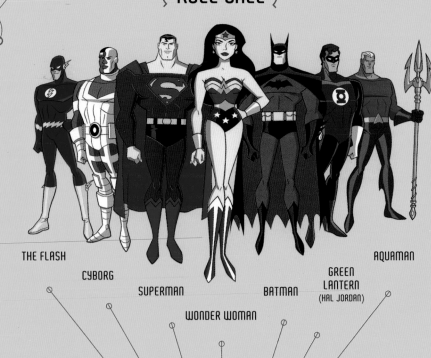

THE FLASH

CYBORG

SUPERMAN

WONDER WOMAN

BATMAN

GREEN
LANTERN
(HAL JORDAN)

AQUAMAN

JUSTICE LEAGUE™

STARRO
AND THE
CYBERSPORE

BY
BRANDON T. SNIDER

ILLUSTRATED BY
TIM LEVINS

raintree

Published by Raintree, an imprint of Capstone Global Library Limited,
a company incorporated in England and Wales having its registered
office at 264 Banbury Road, Oxford, OX2 7DY – Registered company
number: 6695582

www.raintree.co.uk
myorders@raintree.co.uk

STAR39864

ISBN 978 1 4747 4906 0
21 20 19 18 17
10 9 8 7 6 5 4 3 2 1

A full catalogue record for this book is available from the British Library.

Editor: Christopher Harbo
Designer: Bob Lentz
Colourist: Rex Lokus

Printed and bound in China.

MARTIAN
MANHUNTER

HAWKGIRL

HAWKMAN

GREEN ARROW

BLACK CANARY

GREEN LANTERN
(JOHN STEWART)

THE ATOM

SUPERGIRL

RED TORNADO

POWER GIRL

SHAZAM

PLASTIC MAN

BOOSTER GOLD

BLUE BEETLE

ZATANNA

VIXEN

METAMORPHO

ETRIGAN
THE DEMON

FIRESTORM

HUNTRESS

CHAPTER 1

TROUBLE STIRS

The coastal town of Happy Harbor sat on the northernmost tip of the Rhode Island Sound. The local townsfolk considered the Sound to be the perfect place to live because of its lush forests and thriving sea life. It was a quiet place where nothing much happened.

On this day, however, the opposite was true. One of Happy Harbor's outer islands had become a smoking crater. A meteor had unexpectedly crashed, turning the tiny island into a fire pit.

Thankfully, Cyborg had noticed.

As the Justice League's eyes and ears, Cyborg had tracked the small meteor as it entered Earth's orbit. He assumed it would just burn up in the planet's outer atmosphere. When it didn't, Cyborg grew concerned. He tracked the meteor's path and took off to investigate in one of the Justice League's jets.

Arriving on the scene, Cyborg surveyed the area for signs of danger. He made a record of the strange situation for the Justice League's files.

"Cyborg's Logbook: Entry 2865," he began, crouching down to inspect the steamy rubble. "I'm in Happy Harbor, Rhode Island, at the meteor crash site. The crater is about nine metres wide." Cyborg craned his neck over the gaping hole. "And it's deep too."

As he strolled around the edge of the crater, Cyborg used his body's powerful sensors to identify its curious characteristics. "I'm detecting a unique radiation only found in deep space. The crater contains traces of biological life possibly not of this world."

A sudden realization gripped Cyborg. He took a step back to view the scene in full. "This crater forms a crude geometric shape. It looks almost exactly like a star –"

FZZZZZZT!

On the mainland, the lights in Happy Harbor went out, and all electronic devices went dark. Cyborg checked his communication device but couldn't connect to the Justice League's headquarters.

That's not good, he thought.

RUMBLE! RUMBLE! RUMBLE!

The ground shook beneath Cyborg's feet as the crater broke apart.

An earthquake is uncommon for this region, he thought, *but then again so is a giant rock from outer space.*

A series of cracks opened around Cyborg, swallowing the earth he stood on. Before he could get to safety, his systems shut down.

Cyborg lost his footing and fell into the darkness.

* * *

High above the planet in the Watchtower, the Justice League's orbiting headquarters, Green Lantern and The Flash were totally unaware of the danger their teammate faced. They were too busy battling one another for the fate of the universe in the Watchtower's command centre.

"Eat laser, speedster!" Green Lantern exclaimed, tapping the screen on his mobile phone. "Pew pew!"

"HA!" laughed The Flash, swiping his own mobile's screen. "You think a lot of lasers are going to stop *me*, green jeans? I can dodge your blows at the speed of light."

The heroes had been playing a new video game app called *Star Conqueror* for hours. Despite their best efforts, they still hadn't got past the first level. As Batman entered the command centre, Green Lantern and The Flash quickly hid their devices. The World's Greatest Detective wasn't easily fooled.

"*Gentlemen*," Batman said. "You're on monitor duty. Act like it."

"He said *duty*," giggled The Flash. Batman glared with such intensity that the Scarlet Speedster apologized straight away.

"Sorry, Batman," he muttered. "Won't happen again."

"People depend on us to serve and protect them. That requires our full and undivided attention," Batman explained. "Play games in your spare time."

Green Lantern jabbed The Flash in the stomach with his elbow. "Well done for getting us in trouble," he grumped.

"*Me?!*" exclaimed The Flash. "I wasn't the one who wanted to play *Star Conqueror* in the first place! That was *you*, Lantern. Besides, neither of us could even get past the first level. I think that game is rigged."

"*Enough*," Batman said. "Cyborg and I were supposed to meet here to review the Watchtower's newest security procedures. Do you know where he is?"

The Flash and Green Lantern stared at one another in silence.

PING!

A sound from The Flash's game broke the silence. Batman wasn't pleased. *"What's that noise?"* he grimaced.

"Oh, it's nothing, Batman," The Flash said, stuffing the device into a secret pocket on his costume. "Neither of us has seen Cyborg. He's probably doing computer stuff somewhere."

"One of the jets is missing," noted Green Lantern. "Maybe he took it?"

Despite his growing frustration, Batman kept his cool. "Computer. Locate Cyborg," he ordered.

"Justice League Member: Cyborg," the computer responded. "Location: Unknown."

As half-man, half-robot, Cyborg was always connected to the Justice League's network. If the Watchtower's high-tech computer system couldn't find him, something was terribly wrong.

"Computer. Locate all off-site Justice League jets," Batman commanded.

"Jet C-20. Location: Happy Harbor, Rhode Island," the computer replied. Images of the meteor site appeared on the screen. Batman studied every angle. The jet was clearly visible, but Cyborg was nowhere to be found.

"Holy smokes," The Flash said. "What happened there?"

ALERT! ALERT! ALERT!

· The Watchtower's emergency channel sounded off as a red warning light lit up the room.

Batman took control of the situation. He punched a button on the computer.

"This is Batman," he said. "Go ahead."

A concerned face appeared on the monitor above. "Batman, this is Sheriff Harper with the Newport Police Department in Rhode Island," he began. "Something bad is happening at our middle school."

"What's the matter? Did they run out of pizza bagels?" The Flash joked.

"*Quiet,*" whispered Green Lantern. "This sounds serious."

"The kids are going nuts!" Sheriff Harper stammered. "They're attacking anyone who gets in their way. It's like they're zombies or something."

"How are you controlling the situation?" the Dark Knight asked.

"We've got the place surrounded, but these are *kids* we're talking about," explained Sheriff Harper. "We've got to keep them safe, but we're running out of options."

"Stay right where you are. Do not engage," Batman advised. "The League will handle this. Batman out."

"It could be a prank," Green Lantern suggested.

"Only a select few law enforcement officials can use that emergency channel," Batman explained. "Sheriff Harper is one of them. We have to take this seriously."

"Do you want us to check it out, Batman?" asked Green Lantern.

"I've already contacted another Justice League member," advised Batman. "He'll be on the scene within minutes."

"When did you do *that*?" The Flash asked. "I didn't hear you contact anyone."

"I activated an ultrasonic signal that only he can hear. That way, our enemy can't pick up our communications. They won't know we're coming," Batman explained.

"Oh. Good thinking, Batman!" said The Flash. "*Now* I know who you're talking about."

Batman brought up a map of Rhode Island on the monitor. "Happy Harbor, Cyborg's last known whereabouts, is just north of Newport," he said.

"Do you think there's a connection?" Green Lantern asked.

"At this point, we can't rule anything out," Batman said.

* * *

On Earth, the situation inside Newport Middle School grew more dangerous by the second. Pupils ran wild through the corridors, ripping down posters and knocking over rubbish bins.

One boy ran through the library, furiously tipping books off the shelves and cackling with glee. When he reached the non-fiction section of the library, he took a book about great white sharks off the shelf. He flipped it open, ripped out a few pages and stuffed them in his pocket.

WHOOSH!

An unexpected gust of wind blew the damaged book right out of his hands. The boy grabbed a second book about sharks off the shelf.

WHOOSH!

Another gust of wind blew through, sending that book flying as well. The boy became angry and pulled a third shark book off the shelf. He didn't know where the wind came from until he heard a voice from above.

"Books are meant to be read, not destroyed," the voice called out.

The boy looked up. Superman had arrived, and he didn't look pleased.

CHAPTER 2

POSSESSED!

"How about you hand over that book?" Superman asked. The boy threw the book at the Man of Steel and ran away in anger.

Superman had faced many threats in his life as a super hero. He'd fought evil warlords, alien menaces and madmen. But he wasn't sure how to handle a school full of zombified children without hurting them.

He entered the dining room to find pupils overturning tables, hanging from the lights and taking part in a food fight. The chaos stopped for a moment when the pupils realized that the Man of Steel had arrived.

"*Get him!*" a little girl cried out as the angry children ran towards Superman.

I have to be very careful, Superman thought. *If I use my powers too forcefully I could accidentally hurt them.* He took a deep breath and barely puffed his super-breath to push the pupils away from him as he carefully backed out of the dining room. Once outside, he used his heat vision to melt the lock, trapping the pupils inside.

That should hold them for a minute, he thought.

"RARGH!" a boy shouted, surprising Superman from behind. The angry boy jumped on his back as an army of rage-filled children charged down the corridor. They piled on Superman, pounding him with their fists. Despite having unbreakable skin, he could feel incredible power in their blows.

Superman shook off the attack and, at super-speed, dashed to the other end of the school to safety. He used his Justice League communicator to report in.

"This is Superman," he began. "I need a little help down here."

A red and yellow blur whizzed through the corridors, joining the Man of Steel.

"Ta-da!" exclaimed The Flash. "You didn't think we'd leave you hanging, did you?"

BOOM! A glowing, green boxing glove punched through the school's front doors.

"We got here as soon as we could," Green Lantern said.

"Where's Batman?" asked Superman.

"He was right behind me." Green Lantern shrugged and looked over his shoulder. "He's probably off doing his *Batman* thing."

An angry mob of children poured out of every classroom looking for trouble.

"The *conqueror* has awakened us!" screamed one little boy. The other children cheered his words with evil delight, slowly moving towards the heroes.

"Who is the conqueror? You're going to have to be more specific, kid," said Green Lantern. "We've dealt with a lot of criminals in our time."

"Be careful, Green Lantern," warned Superman. "Something sinister has taken hold of these children. Let's not make them any angrier. Be mindful not to hurt them."

"I've got just the thing!" said Green Lantern. He used his ring to create an emerald prison cell which kept the children at bay. "This will do for now, but we're going to need options."

* * *

In a nearby classroom, Batman looked for clues.

Has a virus infected these children? the Dark Knight wondered. *Or is something or someone controlling them?*

As he made his way through the room, he heard whispering. It came from a locked cupboard. Using a pick from his Utility Belt, Batman unlocked the cupboard door and found a teacher huddled in the corner.

"I'm not going to hurt you," he comforted. "You're safe."

"Where are the children?" the teacher asked. "Are they gone?"

"My teammates are making sure they're okay," said Batman. "Take a deep breath, and tell me what happened."

"The children locked me in here!" the teacher began. "It all started when they were coming back from breaktime. One of the boys was playing with his tablet. He'd downloaded a game or something. I'm not quite sure. The other children gathered around in awe. Their eyes were so wide watching whatever was on that thing."

"And then?" asked Batman.

"I told everyone to go back to their seats. Then I asked the boy to turn off his tablet, but he wouldn't," the teacher said, her voice cracking with emotion.

"I know this is difficult," Batman said. "Take me through what happened next."

"He was angry. He began screaming. They all did. Something about a *conqueror* coming to Earth," said the teacher. "I think it had something to do with that stupid game!"

WHOOSH! Suddenly The Flash entered the room. "Found you, Batman," he said.

"Thank you," Batman said to the teacher. He turned his attention to The Flash. "Take her to safety."

The Scarlet Speedster grabbed the teacher and raced her outside, returning in seconds.

"Done!" he said.

"*It's Starro*," Batman growled.

"The giant alien starfish?" asked The Flash. "Starro's got an army of face-hugging, mind-controlling, starfish minions. If he's behind this, then where are they?"

"He doesn't need them anymore," Batman said, activating the *Star Conqueror* app on a nearby tablet. "Not when he's got *this*."

"What the what?!" The Flash exclaimed. "That's my new favourite video game!"

"Starro is using it to control these children," Batman said.

Superman and Green Lantern rushed into the room to join their friends.

"We distracted the kids as best we could. What did we miss?" Green Lantern asked.

"A space starfish is using my favourite app to control kids' minds," said The Flash.

"Huh?" Green Lantern asked.

"Let me explain," Batman began. "Starro has the power to control people's minds. He usually channels his power through smaller versions of himself called spores. They attach themselves to human hosts and take over their bodies. But now he's found a way to use our technology to do the same."

"So, he's finally upgraded, huh? Good for him," The Flash joked.

"This is no laughing matter," Batman growled, showing off the *Star Conqueror* app.

Green Lantern's eyes widened. "That's my game!" he exclaimed.

"Starro is using it to hypnotize children," Batman explained. "He knows humans are attached to mobile devices more than ever before. This app targets specific brain patterns using colours, lights and sounds. Combined with a low frequency pulse, Starro infects the human mind like a virus."

"Why haven't Green Lantern and I been infected by all these lights and sounds?" asked The Flash. "We've been playing that game all day."

"I suspect Starro has fashioned this cyberspore to target developing brains," said Batman. "That's why only children have become infected so far."

"This sounds like the first part of a bigger plan," said Green Lantern.

"That's what I suspect," Batman said. He took a toolkit from his Utility Belt and used it to tinker with the device. "Starro is using a unique frequency to boost the cyberspore. I might be able to rewire this device so that the signal is blocked completely, but it'll take time."

"Be careful, Batman," warned Green Lantern. "One false move, and we all might turn into zombies."

"This technical talk is making my brain hurt," said The Flash.

Superman's enhanced hearing picked up the sound of children rushing down the corridor. They were preparing to launch a new attack. "We don't have much time," he reminded the other heroes.

"Will we have to rewire all the tablets and mobile phones on Earth? We've got our work cut out for us," said Green Lantern.

"Or we find Starro and stop him first," Batman said, pressing buttons on the device.

FZZZZT! Sparks flew from the device. Batman's expression changed, and his mood grew angrier.

"Are you okay?" asked Green Lantern.

"Leave me alone!" Batman exclaimed. He grabbed a flash bomb from his Utility Belt and threw it in Green Lantern's direction.

BOOM! The bomb exploded in a flash of yellow light. When the smoke finally cleared, it was clear that the Dark Knight had fallen under Starro's sinister spell.

"Now Batman's a zombie too," whimpered The Flash. "Can this day get any worse?"

CHAPTER 3

BATMAN ATTACKS!

"Stand back!" Superman shouted. He used his heat vision to melt the tablet in Batman's hands, but it was too late. The Dark Knight had already fallen prey to Starro's mind control. He threw the device on the ground and grunted at his teammates like a beast.

"Now what?" whispered The Flash.

"I know you're still in there, Batman. You have one of the strongest minds I've ever known," Superman said, hoping for a peaceful solution. "*Fight this.* Resist Starro's dark influence. The world needs you."

Batman paused for a moment. It seemed as if he'd heard Superman's plea. Then things took a turn for the worse.

"Bow before the conqueror!" Batman snarled. He opened a lead compartment on his Utility Belt and took out a small piece of Kryptonite. Immediately, the powerful element weakened Superman, and the Man of Steel fell to his knees.

Before The Flash could grab the Kryptonite and throw it away, Batman flung a canister of knockout gas in his direction. It burst in The Flash's face, releasing a mist that knocked him out.

"Uh-oh," Green Lantern said. "I don't want to have to do this, but you leave me no choice." He used his power ring to build an emerald cage around Batman, trapping him in place. "*That* should hold you."

Then Green Lantern turned his attention to the Kryptonite. He created a drone that scooped up the harmful rock and carried it far from Superman.

"Thanks for the save," said Superman.

"You round up the kids, and get them somewhere safe," ordered Green Lantern. "I'll keep an eye on our detective friend."

The Man of Steel rose to his feet and dusted himself off. He was disappointed that he couldn't get through to Batman.

Starro's mind control is more powerful than ever, he thought. *We might be in big trouble.*

Superman zoomed through the school, locating all of the pupils and moving them into the hall. Using his heat vision, he melted the exit doors together to ensure the kids stayed put.

It's for their own safety, the Man of Steel thought.

Meanwhile, Green Lantern rushed over and tried desperately to wake The Flash from his trance.

"Flash! C'mon, buddy," he said, giving his best friend a mild slap on the cheek. "We need you."

"Watch it with the slapping," The Flash groaned. He looked around and was confused. "Why is Batman in a cage? And why can't I move?"

Before Green Lantern could answer, Batman pulled a tiny vial of fear gas out of his Utility Belt. He threw it in Green Lantern's direction, shattering the vial on the ground in front of him. Green Lantern inhaled the gas and felt its effects straight away. His worst fears came alive in front of his eyes.

"Get away! Get away from me!" Green Lantern shouted, stumbling back and forth.

Green Lantern's power ring was only as strong as the will of the person wearing it. As the fear toxin invaded his mind, Green Lantern lost his concentration. Batman's emerald prison evaporated into thin air. The Dark Knight took off towards the hall.

The Flash slowly woke up and vibrated his body at super-speed to burn through the knockout formula. He moved swiftly to help Green Lantern.

"I don't know what that gas is doing to you, Green Lantern, but I've got your back," The Flash said, whipping his arms into a vortex of wind. The cyclone sucked the gas out of Green Lantern's lungs and dissolved it in the air. Green Lantern's mind cleared.

"You okay, buddy?" asked The Flash.

"I'll survive," Green Lantern said, shaking the cobwebs out of his head. "But that fear toxin made me see all kinds of crazy demons and monsters. I need a holiday."

"None of that stuff was real," comforted The Flash. "Once this is all over, we'll find a nice beach somewhere. But for now, we've got work to do."

Superman joined the others. "The kids are safe in the hall. Where's Batman?"

"He escaped," The Flash admitted. "But it's not our fault! That man has some serious tricks up his sleeve."

* * *

At the other end of the school, Batman had reached the hall. He was planning to break the pupils out of their temporary prison.

Before the Dark Knight could act, he became entangled by a golden lasso. Wonder Woman had arrived.

"The Lasso of Truth compels you to fight this sickness, Batman!" she shouted. "I know you can do it."

Batman struggled to free himself from the lasso's magical grip. "Can't stop . . . won't stop . . . the conqueror," he stammered. Batman freed his hand long enough to grab a tiny explosive from his Utility Belt. He threw it at the hall door.

BOOM!

The door exploded into pieces, releasing the pupils from their prison. The commotion distracted Wonder Woman for a moment. It was just long enough for Batman to slip out of the lasso's control and race away from the Amazing Amazon.

Little did Batman know that Wonder Woman had brought a friend.

"Where do you think you're going?" Aquaman asked, blocking Batman's path with his shining trident.

The pupils began pouring into the corridor towards Wonder Woman and Aquaman. Batman used the distraction to duck away through a side door.

"He's a feisty one," Aquaman said. "But it seems we have bigger problems to deal with."

The zombified pupils were closing in fast. The heroes had no choice but to take off on foot to avoid them. As Wonder Woman and Aquaman turned a corner, they were greeted by The Flash and Green Lantern.

"Hi there!" exclaimed The Flash. "Fancy meeting you here!"

"We received a distress call from Superman and came as soon as we could," said Wonder Woman.

As the Justice League raced away from danger, Aquaman had an idea. "I want to try something," he suggested. "I may be able to use my aquatic telepathy to calm the children."

"I thought your power only worked on fish and other marine life," said The Flash.

"Starro is sort of a sea creature. Since the children are linked to him, I might be able to connect to them," Aquaman explained. "Besides, fish and human brains are more alike than you think. All living creatures are part of the animal kingdom."

"So, when Green Lantern tells me I eat like a pig, it's because I've got a little bit of pig in my brain?" asked The Flash. "*Cool.*"

"That's *not* what I said," growled Aquaman. "Stand back and let me work."

"Do your thing, Sea King!" said The Flash.

The zombified children had the Justice League cornered.

"Wonder Woman, I need you to lasso the children. Combined with one of my telepathic blasts, we should be able to slow them for a moment," said Aquaman. "I hope."

Wonder Woman whipped her lasso around a group of zombie pupils. As they struggled to free themselves from its power, Aquaman closed his eyes and concentrated. Using every bit of his mental strength, the King of Atlantis focused his telepathy. The attacking children grew slower and slower. They soon fell asleep and collapsed to the ground.

Aquaman paused to catch his breath. "The children are safe," he explained. "But that took a lot out of me. I don't know how long we have before they wake up."

* * *

At the other end of the school, Superman located Batman and cornered him in the gym. The Man of Steel didn't want to hurt his teammate, but time was running out.

WHOOSH! In an instant, The Flash swiped Batman's Utility Belt and swiftly handed it over to Superman.

"*Now* he won't be able to launch one of his sneaky little attacks," The Flash said.

Green Lantern used his power ring to shackle Batman's hands and legs in a thick tube of green energy. The remaining heroes gathered in the gym to discuss the situation.

"Batman is down, but this school full of kids will still want to destroy us when they wake up," explained Green Lantern. "We need to find Starro and stop him *now*."

Sheriff Harper rushed into the school. He held his mobile up for all to see. An important news bulletin played on its screen. "It's happening everywhere," he said. "Look!"

"*Zombified children are overthrowing governments worldwide,*" the broadcast began. "*We've just received a report that a primary school tour group has even taken over the Rhode Island State Capitol building. More on this as it develops.*"

The news bulletin left the Justice League speechless. The Flash was the first one to break the silence. "This is *bad*," he said.

"Where's Cyborg?" asked Wonder Woman. "We could use his abilities right now."

"He's missing. I have a terrible feeling his disappearance is connected to this whole mess," explained Green Lantern.

"Aquaman and I will search for Cyborg," Wonder Woman said, taking charge of the situation. "The rest of you head to the Rhode Island State Capitol."

Batman struggled to free himself from Green Lantern's emerald shackles, grunting and groaning in anger. "The conqueror will not be stopped," he barked.

"Who's taking Mr. Grumpy Bat?" asked The Flash.

"There's plenty of room for our feisty friend on the Invisible Jet," Wonder Woman said. "Let's go."

CHAPTER 4

TAKEOVER

The Invisible Jet soared across the sky, flying high above the Atlantic Ocean. It headed towards Happy Harbor, Cyborg's last known location. Inside the cockpit, Wonder Woman and Aquaman tried to make sense of their current situation.

"According to Superman, Batman discovered that Starro is controlling these children through a *video game app*," said Wonder Woman, shaking her head. "The modern world is becoming stranger and more dangerous by the day."

"Indeed," Aquaman agreed. "That's why we've got to get to the bottom of this fast. If we don't, we'll be next on Starro's list."

In the back of the jet, Batman began to shake with fury. "Starro will *conquer* this planet," he growled. "You're *nothing* to him."

"C'mon, Aquaman," Wonder Woman said, putting the controls on autopilot. "Let's go have a chat with our guest."

"You are *weak*. The *conqueror* is strong!" Batman shouted, shaking the bars of his cell.

"I've never seen Batman like this," noted Wonder Woman. "Let's see if we can get him to tell us something of value." She looped her lasso through the bars of Batman's prison cell and coiled it around his arm.

"What is Starro planning to do?" she asked. "I'll only ask nicely *once.*"

Batman struggled as Starro's influence grew stronger. "The conqueror wants . . . total control . . . of Earth!" he cried out.

"How does he plan to achieve that goal?" Wonder Woman asked. Her enchanted lasso could make *anyone* tell the truth, but Starro's command ran deep. Batman's mind was in great distress. His body squirmed in torment.

"ARGH!!!" Batman screamed.

"He's fighting," said Wonder Woman. "That's a good sign."

Aquaman wasn't so sure. "The human mind is easily corrupted. Even a great one like *his*," he said. "We have to be very careful here. Starro is dangerous beyond measure."

Batman slumped to the floor, exhausted. Wonder Woman carefully removed her lasso from around his arm.

"We won't let you down, Batman," she whispered. "Keep resisting. I won't stop until we get you back."

Aquaman and Wonder Woman returned to the cockpit to review their plan.

"I don't understand how Starro reached across the planet in such a short amount of time. That requires a massive amount of power," said Aquaman.

Wonder Woman activated the Invisible Jet's holographic map of the Atlantic Ocean. "There's an internet node several kilometres from Happy Harbor," she said. "Starro could be tapping into it directly and using Cyborg to do it."

"If Starro has bonded to Cyborg's advanced circuitry, there's no telling what he's capable of doing," said Aquaman. "We need to get there immediately."

* * *

At the Rhode Island State Capitol, the staff was panicked. They were being terrorized by a group of zombie children. The group had been touring the building on a field trip when Starro attacked. The pupils were told not to bring any mobile devices with them, but one boy didn't listen. He had hidden a mobile phone in his shoe.

No one will stop me from playing Star Conqueror, he had thought.

When the supervising adults turned their backs, the boy showed the phone to his friends. That was when Starro took control. The boy became Starro's general, organizing his classmates against all the adults. The zombified children now held a group of people hostage in the governor's office.

"Where is your leader?" asked the boy.

"Our leader?" asked the tour guide. "I'm not sure what you mean."

"Answer my question!" the boy cackled. "Or the *conqueror* will destroy *everything*."

"You don't want to hurt us do you, kid? That's not very nice," said the tour guide. She shivered with fear. "What's your name?"

"Danny," growled the boy.

The tour guide gulped. "Why are you doing this, Danny?" she murmured. "What happened to you and your friends?"

"*We're* in control now!" the boy barked, pacing back and forth. "And we're going to help the conqueror take over this planet."

The hostages looked at one another in confusion. They didn't know what he meant.

"I am a faithful servant of the *conqueror*!" Danny growled.

Danny stomped his feet in rage as the other children began ripping apart the room. They tore paintings from the walls and knocked over furniture. Danny's eyes darted in all directions, looking for something.

"Where are they?" Danny yelled. "Tell me where they are!"

"Where are *what*?" the tour guide asked. "I don't know what you're talking about."

"You know," Danny growled.

The assembled adults weren't sure what to do. If they said the wrong thing, Danny and his friends might hurt them.

"DO NOT RESIST THE CONQUEROR!" Danny screamed.

A group of children picked up a large wooden desk and threw it against the wall, smashing it to pieces.

Danny's eyes lit up. A black briefcase that had been stuffed under the desk now stood revealed. A voice in his head told him it was filled with weapons, and Danny believed it. The boy had found his prize.

"I finally have the weapons," Danny whispered. *"All hail the conqueror!"* The boy shook the briefcase with fury.

"Weapons? This is just a governor's office. That's a normal briefcase," said the tour guide. She turned to another hostage. "This kid must be losing his mind," she whispered.

"Open it," Danny demanded. *"Now."*

The tour guide gently took the briefcase from the boy. Before she could unlatch it, Superman, The Flash and Green Lantern crashed through the wall of the office. Danny grabbed the briefcase and tried pulling it out of the tour guide's grasp.

The Flash zipped through the room, snatching the briefcase from between them. "If you two can't share, I'm going to have to hold this for you," he said.

"The Justice League! Thank heavens you came! What happened to these poor children?" the tour guide asked.

"Their minds are being controlled," the Man of Steel answered. "They're puppets of an evil being from outer space."

"What's in this thing?" The Flash asked, inspecting the briefcase. "Feels pretty light to me."

Danny pointed at The Flash. "Attack him! For the conqueror!" he shouted.

The children rushed towards The Flash, overwhelming him and wrestling back control of the briefcase.

"Well done, Flash," said Green Lantern.

"What was I supposed to do? I can't hurt a group of kids," The Flash explained. "Even if they *are* attacking me."

The children picked up pieces of broken furniture from inside the governor's office and threw it at the heroes angrily. The Flash and Green Lantern were backed into a corner as Danny ran away with the briefcase.

"Here we go again," Green Lantern said with a sigh.

* * *

In Happy Harbor, Wonder Woman and Aquaman arrived at the meteor crash site where Cyborg was last seen. They carefully inspected the abandoned Justice League jet and the crater, but were unable to find any solid clues.

"The life around this crater has been burned to a crisp," observed Wonder Woman. She looked out to the sea. "The internet node is out there. We should get going."

"Wait a moment, Wonder Woman," said Aquaman. "I want to know exactly what we're getting into." He closed his eyes, cleared his mind, and used his aquatic telepathy to survey the surrounding waters.

"Great Atlantis!" he gasped. "The marine life in this area is scattered and fearful. I'm trying to calm them, but it's difficult. Something terrible is happening down there."

"Then let's go and find out what it is and put an end to it," said Wonder Woman. She put on her diving gear and plunged into the water. Aquaman followed, and the heroic duo made their way through the dark depths of the sea towards the node.

During their journey, Wonder Woman noticed the sparse sea life. "Where are all the beautiful creatures that live among this reef?" she asked.

"They're hiding from something," Aquaman noted.

"Look!" exclaimed Wonder Woman. "Over there!"

Aquaman turned in Wonder Woman's direction to find a shocking sight. Within a deep valley, Starro's enormous starfish body lay draped across a massive internet cable. He was using it to transmit his cyberspore across the planet.

Next to Starro was the zombified Cyborg, whose body was hooked up to the massive electronic system. Starro was using Cyborg's advanced cybernetic abilities to enhance his power.

"We've got to get down there," Wonder Woman said, swimming towards the scene.

"Wait!" shouted Aquaman. He'd spotted two great white sharks emerging from the depths. They'd been outfitted with cybernetic harnesses, complete with laser cannons. The purple glow in their eyes meant they were under Starro's control.

As they swam closer, something else became clear. These sharks were very *hungry*.

CHAPTER 5

STARRO'S LAST STAND

SNAP!

One shark's jaws bit down on Aquaman's golden trident, thrashing it violently from side to side. Under Starro's control, the shark's strength had doubled.

"You're a big, strong boy, aren't you?" Aquaman barked. "But I'm _stronger._" He spun his trident through the water, and flung the dizzy creature away safely.

The other shark fired a series of quick laser blasts in Wonder Woman's direction. The Amazing Amazon spun through the water, dodging each beam with expert skill.

"There's no need for us to harm these great whites. It's that alien menace that's making them behave like this," Aquaman said with disgust.

"I suppose so, but from what I know of sharks, they're not the friendliest of animals to begin with," said Wonder Woman.

"They're territorial creatures," Aquaman said. A light bulb went off in his head. "I've got an idea."

On the sea floor below, Cyborg was busy building a device that would boost Starro's power. His cyberspore would soon spread to every mobile phone, television, computer and cinema screen on the planet. No one would be safe.

I've got to act fast, Aquaman thought. He focused his aquatic telepathy, sending out a strong signal that blanketed the area.

"I'm sure your mental abilities are strong, but these sharks may not listen to orders," said Wonder Woman.

"I'm not communicating with the sharks," Aquaman said. *"Wait for it."*

Multiple pods of dolphins raced through the area, whistling at full volume. The sound drove the cybersharks crazy. The dolphins drove them out to sea, away from Starro and Cyborg.

"A pod of dolphins can be a shark's worst nightmare," Aquaman said.

"Clever." Wonder Woman smiled.

"Don't get too comfortable. They'll be back soon enough. We've got to rescue our friend and save the planet before that happens," Aquaman said with a grin. *"Let's go."*

* * *

At the Rhode Island State Capitol, Superman used his X-ray vision to search for Danny. The boy had taken off on foot.

"You can't hide from me, son," Superman shouted as he walked through the corridors.

As he scanned the building, Superman watched frightened workers hide behind desks and doors. He found Danny rummaging through drawers in a side office. The boy was looking for something.

"Stay back!" Danny shouted. He'd found a Taser and was pointing it in Superman's direction.

"That's not going to hurt me," said Superman.

Danny turned the Taser. He pointed it at a caretaker who was shivering in the corner.

"Do not test the *conqueror*," the boy growled. "He is in *total* control."

The Man of Steel had saved countless lives during his time as a hero. He was an expert at working through tough situations, but this one proved to be uniquely difficult.

The poor boy has no idea what he's doing, Superman thought. *Starro is in complete control of his mind. I must be very careful. If Danny gets upset, he might do something terrible.*

"I need you to put down the Taser," Superman said, standing firm. He used his X-ray vision to see inside the briefcase the boy held under his arm. "That briefcase is just full of papers. It's not whatever Starro wants you to believe it is."

"You're lying," said Danny.

"I'm not," replied Superman. "Don't give in to the conqueror. He's making you believe things that aren't true. *He* doesn't care what happens to you. *I do.* You've got to resist."

Starro was telling Danny's mind one thing and Superman, one of Danny's idols, was telling him another. The situation confused Danny. He wasn't sure what to do anymore and that made him angry.

* * *

In the governor's office, The Flash and Green Lantern had their hands full with the other children. The kids had backed the heroes into a corner and were pelting them with anything they could get their hands on.

"Now would be a good time to zip through the room and do that Flash-y thing you do," nudged Green Lantern.

"I *would*, but I still feel a little woozy from Batman's attack," said The Flash. "Why don't you use that fancy space ring of yours to make something useful instead of yapping away all day?"

Green Lantern released a loud sigh. "I guess I have to do everything," he whispered as his ring glowed brighter.

I've got to be very sneaky about this, he thought. *If those kids see what I'm up to, we're finished.*

Using his power ring, Green Lantern created a long, slithering boa constrictor that quietly coiled itself through the children's legs. Starro's control was so strong it blinded the kids to what was happening around them. Once the snake had twisted itself around the children, it clenched its body, trapping them safely in its coils.

"You've got the most powerful weapon in the universe on your finger, and you come up with a snake?" The Flash cried.

"It's called being careful," said Green Lantern. "You should consider it sometime."

* * *

In the depths of the ocean, Wonder Woman and Aquaman edged closer to destroying Starro's electronic contraption.

"Cyborg's eyes are purple. He's completely under Starro's spell," observed Wonder Woman. "We'll need to free him first if we want any hope of defeating that creature."

"Agreed," Aquaman said.

Cyborg sensed Aquaman and Wonder Woman moving closer. He turned and fired off a sonic blast in their direction.

"Now, Wonder Woman!" Aquaman exclaimed.

The Amazing Amazon corralled Cyborg with her lasso. She swam in circles until the hero was completely wrapped up in a golden cocoon.

"A rope won't stop me," Cyborg growled. "And it won't stop the conqueror!"

"It doesn't have to," said Aquaman with a grin. "We've got more than one trick up our sleeves."

Face to face with Cyborg, the King of Atlantis focused his mental telepathy. He directed every bit of energy he had towards breaking Starro's control. Aquaman knew that the only way to win was to connect directly to Cyborg's human side. He needed to reach Victor Stone.

"Come back to us, Vic!" Aquaman shouted. "I know you're in there. *Resist*, my friend. We need you now more than ever!"

Cyborg struggled to free himself, twisting and turning in the lasso's grip. At last, his body relaxed. Aquaman had broken through Starro's control.

"AHHH!" Cyborg exclaimed, the purple fading from his eyes. Victor Stone was back. "Am I *under water*? Wonder Woman, Aquaman, what's happening?"

RUUUUMBLE!

The sea bed shifted and shook as Starro's enormous starfish body stirred with rage. The creature wasn't pleased that Cyborg had awakened from his spell. Wonder Woman took back her lasso, and the heroes formed a new plan.

"Starro used you to send out his evil cyberspore," explained Aquaman. "Now we need your help to kick him off the planet. I hope you're ready."

"You bet I am," Cyborg exclaimed. "Let's go kick some starfish."

"I need you to boost my telepathy so it reaches across the entire world," Aquaman explained. "Together, we'll release everyone who has fallen prey to Starro's mind control. Then we'll drive that beast back to space."

Aquaman linked his mind with Cyborg's. Cyborg used his sonic cannon to broadcast the telepathic signal across the planet, blocking Starro's cyberspore. The villainous starfish jolted back and forth as he felt his power slipping away. His hideous eye blinked at a rapid pace and his long arms curled in distress.

Starro vibrated uncontrollably as the sonic blast pounded his body. He thrashed from side to side, disconnecting himself from the internet node.

At last, Starro realized his defeat. The ground shook as his monstrous body lifted from the ocean floor. It rose through the water until it reached the surface.

Cyborg used every bit of energy he had to propel the creature out of the water and into the sky. Starro launched himself into space and was out of sight almost immediately.

"*And stay out!*" Cyborg cried.

* * *

At the Rhode Island State Capitol, Danny and his child army snapped back to normal straight away.

"What's happening? What am I doing here?" Danny asked. He stood shivering and frightened. The loss of Starro's mind control left him feeling strange.

"A bad guy took over your mind, but you're safe now, Danny," Superman said as they returned to the governor's office. He turned to the other children and the gathered adults. "You're *all* safe now."

"Thank you, Superman," said the tour guide. "I don't know what we would have done if you and the Justice League hadn't shown up."

Green Lantern, Superman and The Flash helped clear the wreckage from the governor's office. Then they set off to join their teammates in Happy Harbor.

***

Back on the tiny island, Cyborg was making sure the area was safe once again.

"According to my readings, Starro is gone for good," Cyborg said.

Wonder Woman and Aquaman unlocked Batman from his prison cell. They watched as he moved slowly down the steps of the Invisible Jet.

"How are you feeling, Batman," asked Superman.

"I feel like a giant alien starfish invaded my mind," Batman replied, rubbing his head. "But I'll be fine."

"You fought Starro's control bravely," said Wonder Woman. "Like a true warrior."

"So we're not going to talk about the fact that he had a load of stuff in his belt that can hurt us?" shrugged The Flash.

"There's a reason I have defensive measures," Batman began.

"No need to explain," said Superman. "The Justice League is made up of the most powerful beings on the planet. If someone took over *my* mind, there's only one person I'd trust to stop me. That's *you*, Batman."

"Agreed," nodded Aquaman.

"I still don't get why Starro went after kids and not adults," wondered Green Lantern.

"A child's mind is easier to influence," Batman explained. "Starro knew that by corrupting younger minds, he could control them forever. Children are our future. That's why we must protect them so fiercely."

Cyborg slowly raised his hand. "The last thing I remember is investigating a meteor crash. Can someone tell me what I missed?"

"Of course!" The Flash exclaimed.

PING!

"Ooops. That's *me*," said The Flash, taking his mobile phone from a secret pocket on his uniform.

"*No more games*," growled Batman, grabbing The Flash's phone from his hand and placing it in his Utility Belt for safekeeping.

"Awwww, you're no fun," The Flash shrugged. "Happy Harbor certainly looks like a nice place to live. Maybe we should have a secret headquarters here. What do *you* think, Batman?"

"I think you and Green Lantern need to get back to the Watchtower immediately," said Batman. "You've still got monitor duty."

⟨ END ⟩

JL DATABASE: VILLAINS

STARRO

Starro the Conqueror is an enormous starfish creature that stalks planets and enslaves their populations by using powerful mind control. When Starro targets a planet, he usually sends an army of spores down that takes over its citizens and prepares them for total conquest. Starro's spores attach themselves to a person's face. As the spore infects their minds, it places them in a dreamlike state. They have no memory of their actions while under its influence.

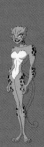

LEX LUTHOR THE JOKER CHEETAH SINESTRO CAPTAIN COLD

BLACK MANTA

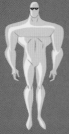

AMAZO

GORILLA GRODD

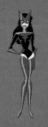

STAR SAPPHIRE

BRAINIAC

DARKSEID

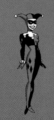

HARLEY QUINN

BIZARRO

THE SHADE

MONGUL

POISON IVY

MR. FREEZE

COPPERHEAD

ULTRA-
HUMANITE

CAPTAIN
BOOMERANG

SOLOMON GRUNDY

BLACK ADAM

DEADSHOT

CIRCE

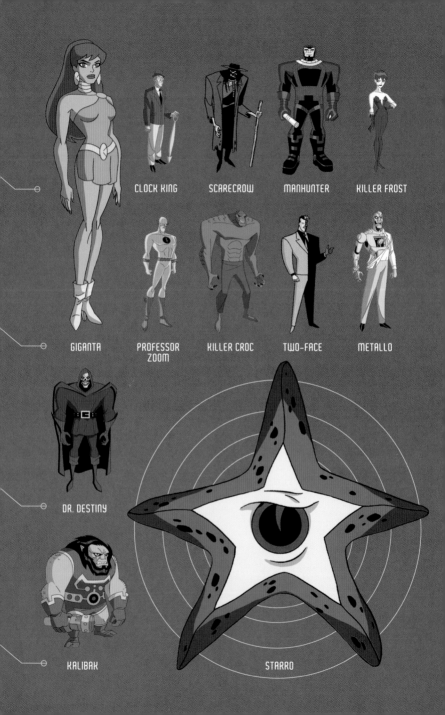

CLOCK KING

SCARECROW

MANHUNTER

KILLER FROST

GIGANTA

PROFESSOR ZOOM

KILLER CROC

TWO-FACE

METALLO

DR. DESTINY

KALIBAK

STARRO

STRENGTH IN NUMBERS

AMAZO AND THE PLANETARY REBOOT
by Brandon T. Snider & Tim Levins

DARKSEID AND THE FIRES OF APOKOLIPS
by Derek Fridolfs & Tim Levins

INJUSTICE GANG AND THE DEADLY NIGHTSHADE
by Derek Fridolfs & Tim Levins

STARRO AND THE CYBERSPORE
by Brandon T. Snider & Tim Levins

raintree
a Capstone company — publishers for children

GLOSSARY

Capitol US government building

conqueror someone who defeats and takes over places or people to rule over them

corrupt make someone bad or dishonest

cybernetic something that is artificial and controlled by computers

frequency number of sound waves that pass a location in a certain amount of time

hypnotize put another person in a sleeplike state

node central connecting point for lines or wires

radiation rays of energy given off by certain elements

spore plant cell that develops into a new plant

telepathy communication from one mind to another without speech or signs

territorial be protective of one's area or land

ultrasonic involving sound waves with frequencies that are too high for humans to hear

vortex air moving in a circular motion

THINK

1. The Flash and Green Lantern play on their mobile devices when they should be on monitor duty. Do you think people spend too much time on their phones or tablets? Discuss your answers.

2. The Flash likes to poke fun at Batman sometimes. Do you poke fun at your friends sometimes? How do they react? Discuss your answer in detail.

3. Batman says a child's mind is easier to influence than an adult's. Do you agree or disagree? Why?

WRITE

1. Starro uses mind control to make people do what he wants. Write a story in which you have mind control powers. What would you get people to do?

2. The Justice League fights Batman when Starro takes over his mind. Have you ever got into an argument with a friend? Write a paragraph describing how you settled your disagreement.

3. Design your own cybershark! What features and abilities does it have? Write a paragraph describing your cybershark. Then draw a picture of it!

AUTHOR

BRANDON T. SNIDER has authored more than 75 books featuring pop culture icons such as Captain Picard, Transformers and the Muppets. He's best known for the top-selling *DC Comics Ultimate Character Guide* and the award-winning *Dark Knight Manual*. Brandon lives in New York City, USA, and is a member of the Writers Guild of America.

ILLUSTRATOR

TIM LEVINS is best known for his work on the Eisner Award-winning DC Comics series *Batman: Gotham Adventures*. Tim has illustrated other DC titles, such as *Justice League Adventures*, *Batgirl*, *Metal Men* and *Scooby-Doo*, and has also done work for Marvel Comics and Archie Comics. Tim enjoys life in Ontario, Canada, with his wife, son, dog and two horses.